DOVER
CHILDREN'S THRIFT CLASSICS

The Boy Who Drew Cats

and Other Japanese Fairy Tales

LAFCADIO HEARN

AND OTHERS

Illustrated by Yuko Green

DOVER PUBLICATIONS, INC.
Mineola, New York

DOVER CHILDREN'S THRIFT CLASSICS
EDITOR OF THIS VOLUME: SUSAN L. RATTINER

Copyright

Published in Canada by General Publishing Company, Ltd., 30 Lesmill Road, Don Mills, Toronto, Ontario.

Published in the United Kingdom by Constable and Company, Ltd., 3 The Lanchesters, 162–164 Fulham Palace Road, London W6 9ER.

Bibliographical Note

The Boy Who Drew Cats and Other Japanese Fairy Tales, first published by Dover Publications, Inc., in 1998, is a new selection of eleven stories originally published in *Japanese Fairy Tales,* Boni and Liveright, Inc., New York, in 1924. The illustrations have been specially prepared for this edition.

Library of Congress Cataloging-in-Publication Data

The boy who drew cats and other Japanese fairy tales / Lafcadio Hearn and others ; illustrated by Yuko Green.
    p.   cm. — (Dover children's thrift classics)
    A new selection of eleven stories originally published in Japanese fairy tales by Boni and Liveright, Inc. in 1924. Illustrations have been specially prepared for this ed.
    Contents: Chin-chin kobakama — The goblin-spider — The old woman who lost her dumplings — The boy who drew cats — The silly jelly-fish — The fountain of youth — The hare of Inaba — My lord bag-o'-rice — The wooden bowl — The tea-kettle — The Matsuyama mirror.
    ISBN 0-486-40348-3 (pbk.)
    1. Fairy   tales—Japan. [1. Fairy   tales. 2. Folklore—Japan.] I. Hearn, Lafcadio, 1850–1904. Japanese fairy tales. II. Green, Yuko, ill. III. Series.
PZ8.B6455   1998
398.2'0952—dc21
                                                  98-23379
                                                              CIP
                                                                AC

Manufactured in the United States of America
Dover Publications, Inc., 31 East 2nd Street, Mineola, N.Y. 11501

Contents

A little Japanese girl takes very good care of her doll.

Chin-Chin Kobakama

THE FLOOR of a Japanese room is covered with beautiful thick soft mats of woven reeds. They fit very closely together, so that you can just slip a knife-blade between them. They are changed once every year, and are kept very clean. The Japanese never wear shoes in the house, and do not use chairs or furniture such as English people use. They sit, sleep, eat, and sometimes even write upon the floor. So the mats must be kept very clean indeed, and Japanese children are taught, just as soon as they can speak, never to spoil or dirty the mats.

Now Japanese children are really very good. All travelers, who have written pleasant books about Japan, declare that Japanese children are much more obedient than English children and much less mischievous. They do not spoil and dirty things, and they do not even break their own toys. A little Japanese girl does not break her doll. No, she takes great care of it, and keeps it even after she becomes a woman and is married. When she becomes a mother, and has a daughter, she gives the doll to that little daughter. And the child takes the same care of the doll that her mother did, and preserves it until she grows up, and gives it at last to her own children, who play with it just as nicely as their grandmother did. So I,—who am writing this little story for you,—have seen in Japan, dolls more than a hundred years old, looking just as pretty as when they

1

were new. This will show you how very good Japanese children are; and you will be able to understand why the floor of a Japanese room is nearly always kept clean,—not scratched and spoiled by mischievous play.

You ask me whether all, *all* Japanese children are as good as that? Well—no, there are a few, a very few naughty ones. And what happens to the mats in the houses of these naughty children? Nothing very bad— because there are fairies who take care of the mats. These fairies tease and frighten children who dirty or spoil the mats. At least—they used to tease and frighten such mischievous children. I am not quite sure whether those little fairies still live in Japan,—because the new railways and the telegraph-poles have frightened a great many fairies away. But here is a little story about them:

Once there was a little girl who was very pretty, but also very lazy. Her parents were rich and had a great many servants; and these servants were very fond of the little girl, and did everything for her which she ought to have been able to do for herself. Perhaps this was what made her so lazy. When she grew up into a beautiful woman, she still remained lazy; but as the servants always dressed and undressed her, and arranged her hair, she looked very charming, and nobody thought about her faults.

At last she was married to a brave warrior, and went away with him to live in another house where there were but few servants. She was sorry not to have as many servants as she had had at home, because she was obliged to do several things for herself, which other folks had always done for her. It was such trouble to her to dress herself, and take care of her own clothes, and keep herself looking neat and pretty to please her husband. But as he was a warrior, and often had to be far away from home with the army, she could sometimes be just as lazy as she wished. Her husband's parents were very old and good-natured, and never scolded her.

Well, one night while her husband was away with the army, she was awakened by queer little noises in her room. By the light of a big paper-lantern she could see very well; and she saw strange things. What?

Hundreds of little men, dressed just like Japanese warriors, but only about one inch high, were dancing all around her pillow. They wore the same kind of dress

Hundreds of little men, only about one inch high,
were dancing all around her pillow.

her husband wore on holidays (*Kamishimo,* a long robe with square shoulders), and their hair was tied up in knots, and each wore two tiny swords. They all looked at her as they danced, and laughed, and they all sang the same song, over and over again:

> *"Chin-chin Kobakama,*
> *Yomo fuké sōro,*
> *Oshizumare, Hime-gimi!*
> *Ya ton ton!"*

Which meant: "We are the Chin-chin Kobakama; the hour is late; sleep, honorable noble darling!"

The words seemed very polite; but she soon saw that the little men were only making cruel fun of her. They also made ugly faces at her.

She tried to catch some of them; but they jumped about so quickly that she could not. Then she tried to drive them away; but they would not go, and they never stopped singing

> *"Chin-chin Kobakama,"*

and laughing at her. Then she knew they were little fairies, and became so frightened that she could not even cry out. They danced around her until morning; then they all vanished suddenly.

She was ashamed to tell anybody what had happened—because, as she was the wife of a warrior, she did not wish anybody to know how frightened she had been.

Next night, again the little men came and danced, and they came also the night after that, and every night—always at the same hour, which the old Japanese used to call the "Hour of the Ox"; that is, about two o'clock in the morning by our time. At last she became very

Her husband, coaxing her gently, asked her what had happened.

sick, through want of sleep and through fright. But the little men would not leave her alone.

When her husband came back home, he was very sorry to find her sick in bed. At first she was afraid to tell him what had made her ill, for fear that he would laugh at her. But he was so kind, and coaxed her so gently, that after a while she told him what happened every night.

He did not laugh at her at all, but looked very serious for a time. Then he asked:

"At what time do they come?"

She answered: "Always at the same hour—the 'Hour of the Ox.'"

"Very well," said her husband, "to-night I shall hide and watch for them. Do not be frightened."

So that night the warrior hid himself in a closet in the sleeping room, and kept watch through a chink between the sliding doors.

He waited and watched until the "Hour of the Ox." Then, all at once, the little men came up through the mats, and began their dance and their song:—

> *"Chin-chin Kobakama,*
> *Yomo fuké sōro."*

They looked so queer, and danced in such a funny way, that the warrior could scarcely keep from laughing. But he saw his young wife's frightened face; and then remembering that nearly all Japanese ghosts and goblins are afraid of a sword, he drew his blade, and rushed out of the closet, and struck at the little dancers. Immediately they all turned into—what do you think?

Toothpicks!

There were no more little warriors—only a lot of old toothpicks scattered over the mats.

The young wife had been too lazy to put her toothpicks away properly; and every day, after having used a new toothpick, she would stick it down between the mats on the floor, to get rid of it. So the little fairies who take care of the floor-mats became angry with her, and tormented her.

Her husband scolded her, and she was so ashamed that she did not know what to do. A servant was called, and the toothpicks were taken away and burned. After that the little men never came back again.

There is also a story told about a lazy little girl, who used to eat plums, and afterward hide the plum-stones between the floor-mats. For a long time she was able to do this without being found out. But at last the fairies got angry and punished her.

For every night, tiny, tiny women—all wearing bright red robes with very long sleeves,—rose up from the floor at the same hour, and danced, and made faces at her and prevented her from sleeping.

Her mother one night sat up to watch, and saw them, and struck at them,—and they all turned into plum-stones! So the naughtiness of that little girl was found out. After that she became a very good girl indeed.

The Goblin-Spider

IN VERY ancient books it is said that there used to be many goblin-spiders in Japan.

Some folks declare there are still some goblin-spiders. During the daytime they look just like common spiders; but very late at night, when everybody is asleep, and there is no sound, they become very, very big, and do awful things. Goblin-spiders are supposed also to have the magical power of taking human shape—so as to deceive people. And there is a famous Japanese story about such a spider.

There was once, in some lonely part of the country, a haunted temple. No one could live in the building because of the goblins that had taken possession of it. Many brave samurai went to that place at various times for the purpose of killing the goblins. But they were never heard of again after they had entered the temple.

At last one who was famous for his courage and his prudence, went to the temple to watch during the night. And he said to those who accompanied him there: "If in the morning I am still alive, I shall drum upon the drum of the temple." Then he was left alone, to watch by the light of a lamp.

As the night advanced he crouched down under the altar, which supported a dusty image of Buddha. He saw nothing strange and heard no sound till after midnight. Then there came a goblin, having but half a body and one eye, and said: *"Hitokusai!"* (There is the smell

8

*Then there came a goblin, having but half a body and one eye,
and said:* "Hitokusai!"

of a man.) But the samurai did not move. The goblin went away.

Then there came a priest and played upon a *samisen* so wonderfully that the samurai felt sure it was not the playing of a man. So he leaped up with his sword drawn. The priest, seeing him, burst out laughing, and said: "So you thought I was a goblin? Oh no! I am only the priest of this temple; but I have to play to keep off the goblins. Does not this *samisen* sound well? Please play a little."

And he offered the instrument to the samurai who grasped it very cautiously with his left hand. But instantly the *samisen* changed into a monstrous spider-web, and the priest into a goblin-spider; and the warrior found himself caught fast in the web by the left hand. He struggled bravely, and struck at the spider with his sword, and wounded it; but he soon became entangled still more in the net, and could not move.

However, the wounded spider crawled away, and the sun rose. In a little while the people came and found the samurai in the horrible web, and freed him. They saw tracks of blood upon the floor, and followed the tracks out of the temple to a hole in the deserted garden. Out of the hole issued a frightful sound of groaning. They found the wounded goblin in the hole, and killed it.

The Old Woman Who Lost Her Dumplings

LONG, LONG ago there was a funny old woman, who liked to laugh and to make dumplings of rice-flour.

One day, while she was preparing some dumplings for dinner, she let one fall; and it rolled into a hole in the earthen floor of her little kitchen and disappeared. The old woman tried to reach it by putting her hand down the hole, and all at once the earth gave way, and the old woman fell in.

She fell quite a distance, but was not a bit hurt; and when she got up on her feet again, she saw that she was standing on a road, just like the road before her house. It was quite light down there; and she could see plenty of rice-fields, but no one in them. How all this happened, I cannot tell you. But it seems that the old woman had fallen into another country.

The road she had fallen upon sloped very much: so, after having looked for her dumpling in vain, she thought that it must have rolled farther away down the slope. She ran down the road to look, crying:

"My dumpling, my dumpling! Where is that dumpling of mine?"

After a little while she saw a stone *Jizō* standing by the roadside, and she said:

"O Lord *Jizō*, did you see my dumpling?" *Jizō* answered:

"Yes, I saw your dumpling rolling by me down the road.

11

But you had better not go any farther, because there is a wicked *Oni* living down there, who eats people."

But the old woman only laughed, and ran on further down the road, crying: "My dumpling, my dumpling! Where is that dumpling of mine?" And she came to another statue of *Jizō,* and asked it:

"O kind Lord *Jizō,* did you see my dumpling?"

And *Jizō* said:

"Yes, I saw your dumpling go by a little while ago. But you must not run any further, because there is a wicked *Oni* down there, who eats people."

But she only laughed, and ran on, still crying out: "My dumpling, my dumpling! Where is that dumpling of mine?" And she came to a third *Jizō,* and asked it:

"O dear Lord *Jizō,* did you see my dumpling?"

But *Jizō* said:

"Don't talk about your dumpling now. Here is the *Oni* coming. Squat down here behind my sleeve, and don't make any noise."

Presently the *Oni* came very close, and stopped and bowed to *Jizō,* and said:

"Good-day, *Jizō San!"*

Jizō said good-day, too, very politely.

Then the *Oni* suddenly snuffed the air two or three times in a suspicious way, and cried out: *"Jizō San, Jizō San!* I smell a smell of mankind somewhere—don't you?"

"Oh!" said *Jizō,* "perhaps you are mistaken."

"No, no!" said the *Oni* after snuffing the air again, "I smell a smell of mankind."

Then the old woman could not help laughing—*"Te-he-he!"*—and the *Oni* immediately reached down his big hairy hand behind *Jizō's* sleeve, and pulled her out, still laughing, *"Te-he-he!"*

"Ah! ha!" cried the *Oni.*

The Oni *reached down his big hairy hand and pulled the old woman out, still laughing,* "Te-he-he!"

Then *Jizō* said:

"What are you going to do with that good old woman? You must not hurt her."

"I won't," said the *Oni*. "But I will take her home with me to cook for us."

"Te-he-he!" laughed the old woman.

"Very well," said *Jizō;* "but you must really be kind to her. If you are not, I shall be very angry."

"I won't hurt her at all," promised the *Oni;* "and she will only have to do a little work for us every day. Good-by, *Jizō San.*"

Then the *Oni* took the old woman far down the road, till they came to a wide deep river, where there was a boat. He put her into the boat, and took her across the river to his house. It was a very large house. He led her

at once into the kitchen, and told her to cook some dinner for himself and the other *Oni* who lived with him.
And he gave her a small wooden rice-paddle, and said:

"You must always put only one grain of rice into the
pot, and when you stir that one grain of rice in the

*Every time she moved the paddle the rice increased in quantity;
and in a few minutes the great pot was full.*

water with this paddle, the grain will multiply until the
pot is full."

So the old woman put just one rice-grain into the pot,
as the *Oni* told her, and began to stir it with the paddle;
and, as she stirred, the one grain became two,—then
four,—then eight,—then sixteen, thirty-two, sixty-four,
and so on. Every time she moved the paddle the rice

increased in quantity; and in a few minutes the great pot was full.

After that, the funny old woman stayed a long time in the house of the *Oni,* and every day cooked food for him and for all his friends. The *Oni* never hurt or frightened her, and her work was made quite easy by the magic paddle—although she had to cook a very, very great quantity of rice, because an *Oni* eats much more than any human being eats.

But she felt lonely, and always wished very much to go back to her own little house, and make her dumplings. And one day, when the *Oni* were all out somewhere, she thought she would try to run away.

She first took the magic paddle, and slipped it under her girdle; and then she went down to the river. No one saw her; and the boat was there. She got into it, and pushed off; and as she could row very well, she was soon far away from the shore.

But the river was very wide; and she had not rowed more than one-fourth of the way across, when the *Oni,* all of them, came back to the house.

They found that their cook was gone, and the magic paddle, too. They ran down to the river at once, and saw the old woman rowing away very fast.

Perhaps they could not swim: at all events they had no boat; and they thought the only way they could catch the funny old woman would be to drink up all the water of the river before she got to the other bank. So they knelt down, and began to drink so fast that before the old woman had got half way over, the water had become quite low.

But the old woman kept on rowing until the water had got so shallow that the *Oni* stopped drinking, and began to wade across. Then she dropped her oar, took the magic paddle from her girdle, and shook it at the

*She sold her dumplings to her neighbors and passengers,
and soon became rich.*

Oni, and made such funny faces that the *Oni* all burst out laughing.

But the moment they laughed, they could not help throwing up all the water they had drunk, and so the river became full again. The *Oni* could not cross; and the funny old woman got safely over to the other side, and ran away up the road as fast as she could.

She never stopped running until she found herself at home again.

After that she was very happy; for she could make dumplings whenever she pleased. Besides, she had the magic paddle to make rice for her. She sold her dumplings to her neighbors and passengers, and in quite a short time she became rich.

The Boy Who Drew Cats

A LONG, long time ago, in a small country-village in Japan, there lived a poor farmer and his wife, who were very good people. They had a number of children, and found it very hard to feed them all. The elder son was strong enough when only fourteen years old to help his father; and the little girls learned to help their mother almost as soon as they could walk.

But the youngest child, a little boy, did not seem to be fit for hard work. He was very clever,—cleverer than all his brothers and sisters; but he was quite weak and small, and people said he could never grow very big. So his parents thought it would be better for him to become a priest than to become a farmer. They took him with them to the village-temple one day, and asked the good old priest who lived there, if he would have their little boy for his acolyte, and teach him all that a priest ought to know.

The old man spoke kindly to the lad, and asked him some hard questions. So clever were the answers that the priest agreed to take the little fellow into the temple as an acolyte, and to educate him for the priesthood.

The boy learned quickly what the old priest taught him, and was very obedient in most things. But he had one fault. He liked to draw cats during study-hours, and to draw cats even where cats ought not to have been drawn at all.

18

Whenever the boy found himself alone, he drew cats.

Whenever he found himself alone, he drew cats. He drew them on the margins of the priest's books, and on all the screens of the temple, and on the walls, and on the pillars. Several times the priest told him this was not right; but he did not stop drawing cats. He drew them because he could not really help it. He had what is called "the genius of an *artist*," and just for that reason he was not quite fit to be an acolyte;—a good acolyte should study books.

One day after he had drawn some very clever pictures of cats upon a paper screen, the old priest said to him severely: "My boy, you must go away from this temple at once. You will never make a good priest, but perhaps you will become a great artist. Now let me give you a last piece of advice, and be sure you never forget it. *Avoid large places at night;—keep to small!*"

The boy did not know what the priest meant by saying, *"Avoid large places;—keep to small."* He thought and thought, while he was tying up his little bundle of clothes to go away; but he could not understand those words, and he was afraid to speak to the priest any more, except to say good-by.

He left the temple very sorrowfully, and began to wonder what he should do. If he went straight home he felt sure his father would punish him for having been disobedient to the priest: so he was afraid to go home. All at once he remembered that at the next village, twelve miles away, there was a very big temple. He had heard there were several priests at that temple; and he made up his mind to go to them and ask them to take him for their acolyte.

Now that big temple was closed up but the boy did not know this fact. The reason it had been closed up was that a goblin had frightened the priests away, and had taken possession of the place. Some brave war-

riors had afterward gone to the temple at night to kill
the goblin; but they had never been seen alive again.
Nobody had ever told these things to the boy;—so he
walked all the way to the village hoping to be kindly
treated by the priests.

When he got to the village it was already dark, and all
the people were in bed; but he saw the big temple on a
hill at the other end of the principal street, and he saw
there was a light in the temple. People who tell the
story say the goblin used to make that light, in order to
tempt lonely travelers to ask for shelter. The boy went
at once to the temple, and knocked. There was no
sound inside. He knocked and knocked again; but still
nobody came. At last he pushed gently at the door, and
was quite glad to find that it had not been fastened. So
he went in, and saw a lamp burning,—but no priest.

He thought some priest would be sure to come very
soon, and he sat down and waited. Then he noticed
that everything in the temple was gray with dust, and
thickly spun over with cobwebs. So he thought to himself that the priests would certainly like to have an
acolyte, to keep the place clean. He wondered why they
had allowed everything to get so dusty. What most
pleased him, however, were some big white screens,
good to paint cats upon. Though he was tired, he
looked at once for a writing-box, and found one, and
ground some ink, and began to paint cats.

He painted a great many cats upon the screens; and
then he began to feel very, very sleepy. He was just on
the point of lying down to sleep beside one of the
screens, when he suddenly remembered the words,
"Avoid large places;—keep to small!"

The temple was very large; he was all alone; and as
he thought of these words,—though he could not quite
understand them—he began to feel for the first time a

little afraid; and he resolved to look for a *small place* in which to sleep. He found a little cabinet, with a sliding door, and went into it, and shut himself up. Then he lay down and fell fast asleep.

Very late in the night he was awakened by a most terrible noise,—a noise of fighting and screaming. It was so dreadful that he was afraid even to look through a chink of the little cabinet: he lay very still, holding his breath for fright.

The light that had been in the temple went out; but the awful sounds continued, and became more awful, and all the temple shook. After a long time silence

Then he saw, lying dead in the middle of the floor,
an enormous, monstrous rat,—a goblin-rat.

came; but the boy was still afraid to move. He did not move until the light of the morning sun shone into the cabinet through the chinks of the little door.

Then he got out of his hiding-place very cautiously, and looked about. The first thing he saw was that all the floor of the temple was covered with blood. And then he saw, lying dead in the middle of it, an enormous, monstrous rat,—a goblin-rat,—bigger than a cow!

But who or what could have killed it? There was no man or other creature to be seen. Suddenly the boy observed that the mouths of all the cats he had drawn the night before, were red and wet with blood. Then he knew that the goblin had been killed by the cats which he had drawn. And then also, for the first time, he understood why the wise old priest had said to him, *"Avoid large places at night;—keep to small."*

Afterward that boy became a very famous artist. Some of the cats which he drew are still shown to travelers in Japan.

The Silly Jelly-Fish

ONCE UPON a time the King of the Dragons, who had till then lived as a bachelor, took it into his head to get married. His bride was a young Dragonette just sixteen years old,—lovely enough, in very sooth, to become the wife of a King. Great were the rejoicings on the occasion. The Fishes, both great and small, came to pay their respects, and to offer gifts to the newly wedded pair; and for some days all was feasting and merriment.

But alas! even Dragons have their trials. Before a month had passed, the young Dragon Queen fell ill. The doctors dosed her with every medicine that was known to them, but all to no purpose. At last they shook their heads, declaring that there was nothing more to be done. The illness must take its course, and she would probably die. But the sick Queen said to her husband:

"I know of something that will cure me. Only fetch me a live Monkey's liver to eat, and I shall get well at once." "A live Monkey's liver!" exclaimed the King. "What are you thinking of, my dear? Why! you forget that we Dragons live in the sea, while Monkeys live far away from here, among the forest-trees on land. A Monkey's liver! Why! darling, you must be mad." Hereupon the young Dragon Queen burst into tears: "I only ask you for one small thing," whimpered she, "and you won't get it for me. I always thought you didn't really love me. Oh! I wish I had stayed at home with my own m-m-m-

24

mamma and my own papa-a-a-a!" Here her voice choked with sobs, and she could say no more.

Well, of course the Dragon King did not like to have it thought that he was unkind to his beautiful young wife. So he sent for his trusty servant the Jelly-Fish, and said: "It is rather a difficult job; but what I want you to try to do is to swim across to the land, and persuade a live Monkey to come here with you. In order to make the Monkey willing to come, you can tell him how much nicer everything is here in Dragon-Land than away where he lives. But what I really want him for is to cut out his liver, and use it as medicine for your young Mistress, who, as you know, is dangerously ill."

So the Jelly-Fish went off on his strange errand. In those days he was just like any other fish, with eyes, and fins, and a tail. He even had little feet, which made him able to walk on the land as well as to swim in the water. It did not take him many hours to swim across to the country where the Monkeys lived; and fortunately there just happened to be a fine Monkey skipping about among the branches of the trees near the place where the Jelly-Fish landed. So the Jelly-Fish said: "Mr. Monkey! I have come to tell you of a country far more beautiful than this. It lies beyond the waves, and is called Dragon-Land. There is pleasant weather there all the year round, there is always plenty of ripe fruit on the trees, and there are none of those mischievous creatures called Men. If you will come with me, I will take you there. Just get on my back."

The Monkey thought it would be fun to see a new country. So he leapt onto the Jelly-Fish's back, and off they started across the water. But when they had gone about half-way, he began to fear that perhaps there might be some hidden danger. It seemed so odd to be fetched suddenly in that way by a stranger. So he said

The Monkey bounded off the Jelly-Fish's back,
and up to the topmost branch of the tree.

to the Jelly-Fish: "What made you think of coming for me?" The Jelly-Fish answered: "My Master, the King of the Dragons, wants you in order to cut out your liver, and give it as medicine to his wife, the Queen, who is sick."

"Oh! that's your little game,—is it?" thought the Monkey. But he kept his thoughts to himself, and only said: "Nothing could please me better than to be of service to Their Majesties. But it so happens that I left my liver hanging to a branch of that big chestnut-tree, which you found me skipping about on. A liver is a thing that weighs a good deal. So I generally take it out, and play about without it during the daytime. We must go back for it." The Jelly-Fish agreed that there was nothing else to be done under the circumstances. For,—silly creature that he was,—he did not see that the Monkey was telling a story in order to avoid getting killed, and having his liver used as medicine for the fanciful young Dragon Queen.

When they reached the shore of Monkey-Land again, the Monkey bounded off the Jelly-Fish's back, and up to the topmost branch of the chestnut-tree in less than no time. Then he said: "I do not see my liver here. Perhaps somebody has taken it away. But I will look for it. You, meantime, had better go back and tell your Master what has happened. He might be anxious about you, if you did not get home before dark."

So the Jelly-Fish started off a second time; and when he got home, he told the Dragon King everything just as it had happened. But the King flew into a passion with him for his stupidity, and hallooed to his officers, saying: "Away with this fellow! Take him, and beat him to a jelly! Don't let a single bone remain unbroken in his body!" So the officers seized him, and beat him, as the King had commanded. That is the reason why, to this very day, Jelly-Fishes have no bones, but are just nothing more than a mass of pulp.

As for the Dragon Queen, when she found she could not have the Monkey's liver,—why! she made up her mind that the only thing to do was to get well without it.

The Fountain of Youth

LONG, LONG ago there lived somewhere among the mountains of Japan a poor woodcutter and his wife. They were very old, and had no children. Every day the husband went alone to the forest to cut wood, while the wife sat weaving at home.

One day the old man went further into the forest than was his custom, to seek a certain kind of wood; and he suddenly found himself at the edge of a little spring he had never seen before. The water was strangely clear and cold, and he was thirsty; for the day was hot, and he had been working hard. So he doffed his huge straw-hat, knelt down, and took a long drink.

That water seemed to refresh him in a most extraordinary way. Then he caught sight of his own face in the spring, and started back. It was certainly his own face, but not at all as he was accustomed to see it in the bronze mirror at home. It was the face of a very young man! He could not believe his eyes. He put up both hands to his head which had been quite bald only a moment before, when he had wiped it with the little blue towel he always carried with him. But now it was covered with thick black hair. And his face had become smooth as a boy's: every wrinkle was gone. At the same moment he discovered himself full of new strength. He stared in astonishment at the limbs that had been so long withered by age: they were now shapely and hard with dense young muscle. Unknowingly he had drunk of the Fountain of Youth; and that draught had transformed him.

*He caught sight of his own youthful face in the spring,
and could not believe his eyes.*

First he leaped high and shouted for joy;—then he ran home faster than he had ever run before in his life. When he entered his house his wife was frightened;—because she took him for a stranger; and when he told her the wonder, she could not at once believe him. But after a long time he was able to convince her that the young man she now saw before her was really her husband; and he told her where the spring was, and asked her to go there with him.

Then she said:—"You have become so handsome and so young that you cannot continue to love an old woman;—so I must drink some of that water immediately. But it will never do for both of us to be away from the house at the same time. Do you wait here, while I go." And she ran to the woods all by herself.

She found the spring and knelt down, and began to drink. Oh! how cool and sweet that water was! She drank and drank and drank, and stopped for breath only to begin again.

Her husband waited for her impatiently;—he expected to see her come back changed into a pretty slender girl. But she did not come back at all. He got anxious, shut up the house, and went to look for her.

When he reached the spring, he could not see her. He was just on the point of returning when he heard a little wail in the high grass near the spring. He searched there and discovered his wife's clothes and a baby,—a very small baby, perhaps six months old.

For the old woman had drunk too deeply of the magical water; she had drunk herself far back beyond the time of youth into the period of speechless infancy.

He took up the child in his arms. It looked at him in a sad wondering way. He carried it home,—murmuring to it,—thinking strange melancholy thoughts.

The Hare of Inaba

NOW, THERE were once eighty-one brothers, who were Princes in the land. They were all jealous of one another, each one wishing to be King, to rule over the others, and over the whole Kingdom. Besides this, each one wanted to marry the same Princess. She was the Princess of Yakami in Inaba.

At last they made up their minds that they would go together to Inaba, and each one try to persuade the Princess to marry him. Although eighty of these brothers were jealous of one another, yet they all agreed in hating, and being unkind to the eighty-first, who was good and gentle, and did not like their rough, quarrelsome ways. When they set out upon their journey, they made the poor eighty-first brother walk behind them, and carry the bag, just as if he had been their servant, although he was their own brother, and as much a Prince as any of them all.

By and by, the eighty Princes came to Cape Keta, and there they found a poor hare, with all his fur plucked out, lying down very sick and miserable. The eighty Princes said to the hare:

"We will tell you what you should do. Go and bathe in the sea water, and then lie down on the slope of a high mountain, and let the wind blow upon you. That will soon make your fur grow, we promise you."

So the poor hare believed them, and went and bathed in the sea, and afterwards lay down in the sun

31

and the wind to dry. But, as the salt water dried, the skin of his body all cracked and split with the sun and the wind, so that he was in terrible pain, and lay there crying, in a much worse state than he was before.

Now the eighty-first brother was a long way behind the others, because he had the luggage to carry, but at

When he saw the hare he asked: "Why are you lying there crying?"

last he came up staggering under the weight of the heavy bag. When he saw the hare he asked:

"Why are you lying there crying?"

"Oh dear!" said the hare, "just stop a moment and I will tell you all my story. I was in the island of Oki, and I wanted to cross over to this land. I didn't know how to

get over, but at last I hit upon a plan. I said to the crocodiles:

"'Let us count how many crocodiles there are in the
sea, and how many hares there are in the land. And now
to begin with the crocodiles. Come, every one of you,
and lie down in a row, across from this island to Cape
Keta, then I will step upon each one, and count you as
I run across. When I have finished counting you, we can
count the hares, and then we shall know whether there
are most hares, or most crocodiles.'

"The crocodiles came and lay down in a row. Then I
stepped on them and counted them as I ran across, and
was just going to jump on shore, when I laughed and
said, 'You silly crocodiles, I don't care how many of you
there are. I only wanted a bridge to get across by.' Oh!
why did I boast until I was safe on dry land? For the last
crocodile, the one which lay at the very end of the row,
seized me, and plucked off all my fur."

"And serve you right too, for being so tricky," said
the eighty-first brother. "However, go on with your
story."

"As I was lying here crying," continued the hare, "the
eighty Princes who went by before you, told me to
bathe in salt water, and lie down in the wind. I did as
they told me, but I am ten times worse than before, and
my whole body is smarting and sore."

Then the eighty-first brother said to the hare, "Go
quickly now to the river, it is quite near. Wash yourself
well with the fresh water, then take the pollen of the
sedges growing on the river bank, spread it about on
the ground, and roll among it; if you do this, your skin
will heal, and your fur grow again."

So the hare did as he was told; and this time he was
quite cured, and his fur grew thicker than ever.

Then the hare said to the eighty-first brother, "As for

those eighty Princes, your brothers, they shall not get the Princess of Inaba. Although you carry the bag, yet your Highness shall at last get both the princess and the country."

Which things came to pass, for the Princess would have nothing to do with those eighty bad brothers, but chose the eighty-first who was kind and good. Then he was made King of the country, and lived happily all his life.

My Lord Bag-o'-Rice

ONCE UPON a time there was a brave warrior, called My Lord Bag-o'-Rice, who spent all his time in waging war against the King's enemies.

One day, when he had sallied forth to seek adventures, he came to an immensely long bridge, spanning a river just at the place where it flowed out of a fine lake. When he set foot on this bridge, he saw that a Serpent twenty feet long was lying there basking in the sun, in such a way that he could not cross the bridge without treading on it.

Most men would have taken to their heels at so frightful a sight. But My Lord Bag-o'-Rice was not to be daunted. He simply walked right ahead,—squash, scrunch, over the Serpent's body.

Instantly the Serpent turned into a tiny Dwarf, who, humbly bowing the knee, and knocking the planks of the bridge three times with his head in token of respect, said: "My Lord! you are a man, you are! For many a weary day have I lain here, waiting for one who should avenge me on my enemy. But all who saw me were cowards, and ran away. You will avenge me, will you not? I live at the bottom of this lake, and my enemy is a Centipede who dwells at the top of yonder mountain. Come along with me, I beseech you. If you help me not, I am undone."

The Warrior was delighted at having found such an adventure as this. He willingly followed the Dwarf to his summer-house beneath the waters of the lake. It was all curiously built of coral and metal sprays in the shape of sea-weed and other water-plants, with freshwater crabs as big as men, and water-monkeys, and newts, and tadpoles as servants and bodyguards. When they had rested awhile, dinner was brought in on trays shaped like the leaves of water-lilies. The dishes were watercress leaves,—not real ones, but much more beautiful than real ones; for they were of water-green porcelain with a shimmer of gold; and the chop-sticks were of beautiful petrified wood like black ivory. As for the wine in the cups, it *looked* like water; but, as it *tasted* all right, what did its looks signify?

Well, there they were, feasting and singing; and the Dwarf had just pledged the Warrior in a goblet of hot steaming wine, when thud! thud! thud! like the tramp of an army, the fearful monster of whom the Dwarf had spoken was heard approaching. It sounded as if a continent were in motion; and on either side there seemed to be a row of a thousand men with lanterns. But the Warrior was able to make out, as the danger drew nearer, that all this fuss was made by a single creature, an enormous Centipede over a mile long; and that what had seemed like men with lanterns on either side of it, were in reality its own feet, of which it had exactly one thousand on each side of its body, all of them glistening and glinting with the sticky poison that oozed out of every pore.

There was no time to be lost. The Centipede was already half-way down the mountain. So the Warrior snatched up his bow, a bow so big and heavy that it would have taken five ordinary men to pull it,—fitted an arrow into the bow-notch, and let fly.

He was not one ever to miss his aim. The arrow struck right in the middle of the monster's forehead.

But alas! it rebounded as if that forehead had been made of brass.

A second time did the Warrior take his bow and shoot. A second time did the arrow strike and rebound; and now the dreadful creature was down to the water's edge, and would soon pollute the lake with its filthy poison. Said the Warrior to himself: "Nothing kills Centipedes so surely as human spittle." And with these words, he spat on to the tip of the only arrow that remained to him (for there had been but three in his quiver). This time again the arrow hit the Centipede right in the middle of its forehead. But instead of rebounding, it went right in and came out again at the back of the creature's head, so that the Centipede fell

A second time did the Warrior take his bow and shoot.

down dead, shaking the whole country-side like an earthquake, and the poisonous light on its two thousand feet darkening to a dull glare like that of the twilight of a stormy day.

Then the Warrior found himself wafted back to his own castle; and round him stood a row of presents, on each of which were inscribed the words "From your grateful dwarf." One of these presents was a large bronze bell, which the Warrior, who was a religious man as well as a brave one, hung up in the temple that contained the tombs of his ancestors. The second was a sword, which enabled him ever after to gain the victory over all his enemies. The third was a suit of armor which no arrow could penetrate. The fourth was a roll of silk, which never grew smaller, though he cut off large pieces from time to time to make himself a new court dress.

The fifth was a bag of rice, which, though he took from it day after day for meals for himself, his family, and his trusty retainers, never got exhausted as long as he lived.

And it was from this fifth and last present that he took his name and title of "My Lord Bag-o'-Rice"; for all the people thought that there was nothing stranger in the whole world than this wonderful bag, which made its owner such a rich and happy man.

The Wooden Bowl

ONCE UPON a time there lived an old couple who had seen better days. Formerly they had been well to do, but misfortune came upon them, through no fault of their own, and in their old age they had become so poor that they were only just able to earn their daily bread.

One joy, however, remained to them. This was their only child, a good and gentle maiden, of such wonderful beauty that in all that land she had no equal.

At length the father fell sick and died, and the mother and her daughter had to work harder than ever. Soon the mother felt her strength failing her, and great was her sorrow at the thought of leaving her child alone in the world.

The beauty of the maiden was so dazzling that it became the cause of much thought and anxiety to the dying mother. She knew that in one so poor and friendless as her child it would be likely to prove a misfortune instead of a blessing.

Feeling her end to be very near, the mother called the maiden to her bedside, and, with many words of love and warning, entreated her to continue pure and good and true, as she had ever been. She told her that her beauty was a perilous gift which might become her ruin, and commanded her to hide it, as much as possible, from the sight of all men.

That she might do this the better the mother placed on her daughter's head a lacquered wooden bowl, which she warned her on no account to take off. The bowl overshadowed the maiden's face, so that it was impossible to tell how much beauty was hidden beneath it.

After her mother's death the poor child was, indeed, forlorn; but she had a brave heart, and at once set about earning her living by hard work in the fields.

As she was never seen without the wooden bowl, which, indeed, appeared a very funny head-dress, she soon began to be talked about, and was known in all the country round as the Maid with the Bowl on her Head.

She was known in all the country round
as the Maid with the Bowl on her Head.

Proud and bad people scorned and laughed at her, and the idle young men of the village made fun of her, trying to peep under the bowl, and even to pull it off her head. But it seemed firmly fixed, and none of them succeeded in taking it off, or in getting more than a glimpse of the beautiful face beneath.

The poor girl bore all this rude usage patiently, was always diligent at her work, and when evening came crept quietly to her lonely home. Now, one day, when she was at work in the harvest field of a rich farmer, who owned most of the land in that part, the master himself drew near. He was struck by the gentle and modest behavior of the young girl, and by her quickness and diligence at her work.

Having watched her all that day, he was so much pleased with her that he kept her in work until the end of the harvest. After that, winter having now come on, he took her into his own house to wait upon his wife, who had long been sick, and seldom left her bed.

Now the poor orphan had a happy home once more, for both the farmer and his wife were very kind to her. As they had no daughter of their own, she became more like the child of the house than a hired servant. And, indeed, no child could have made a gentler or more tender nurse to a sick mother than did this little maid to her mistress.

After some time the master's eldest son came home on a visit to his father and mother. He had been living in Kyoto, the rich and gay city of the Mikado, where he had studied and learned much. Wearied with feasting and pleasure, he was glad to come back for a little while to the quiet home of his childhood. But week after week passed, and, to the surprise of his friends, he showed no desire to return to the more stirring life of the town.

The truth is, that no sooner had he set eyes on the

Maid with the Bowl on her Head than he was filled with curiosity to know all about her. He asked who and what she was, and why she was always seen with such a curious and unbecoming head-dress.

He was touched by her sad story, but could not help laughing at her odd fancy of wearing the bowl on her

He fell deeply in love with her
and vowed to make the Maid with the Bowl his wife.

head. But, as he saw day by day her goodness and gentle manners, he laughed no more. And one day, having managed to take a sly peep under the bowl, he saw enough of her beauty to make him fall deeply in love with her. From that moment he vowed that none other than the Maid with the Bowl should be his wife. His relations, however, would not hear of the match. "No doubt the girl was all very well in her way," they said, "but after all she was only a servant, and no fit mate for the son of the house." They had always said she was being made too much of, and would one day or another turn against her benefactors. Now their words were coming true, and besides, why did she persist in wearing that ridiculous thing on her head? Doubtless to get a reputation for beauty, which most likely she did not possess. Indeed, they were almost certain that she was quite plain-looking.

The two old maiden aunts of the young man were especially bitter, and never lost an opportunity of repeating the hard and unkind things which were said about the poor orphan. Her mistress even, who had been so good to her, now seemed to turn against her, and she had no friend left except her master, who would really have been pleased to welcome her as his daughter, but did not dare to say as much. The young man, however, remained firm to his purpose. As for all the stories which they brought him, he gave his aunts to understand that he considered them little better than a pack of ill-natured inventions.

At last, seeing him so steadfast in his determination, and that their opposition only made him the more obstinate, they were fain to give in, though with a bad grace.

A difficulty now arose where it was least to have been expected. The poor little Maid with the Bowl on her Head upset all their calculations by gratefully, but firmly, refusing the hand of her master's son, and no persuasion on his part could induce her to change her mind.

Great was the astonishment and anger of the relations. That they should be made fools of in this way was beyond all bearing. What did the ungrateful young minx expect; that her master's son wasn't good enough for her? Little did they know her true and loyal heart. She loved him dearly, but she would not bring discord and strife into the home which had sheltered her in her poverty; for she had marked the cold looks of her mistress, and very well understood what they meant. Rather than bring trouble into that happy home she would leave it at once, and for ever. She told no one, and shed many bitter tears in secret, yet she remained true to her purpose. Then, that night when she had cried herself to sleep, her mother appeared to her in a dream, and told her that she might, without scruple, yield to the prayers of her lover and to the wishes of her own heart. She woke up full of joy, and when the young man once more entreated her she answered yes, with all her heart. "We told you so," said the mother and the aunts, but the young man was too happy to mind them. So the wedding-day was fixed, and the grandest preparations were made for the feast. Some unpleasant remarks were doubtless to be heard about the beggar maid and her wooden bowl, but the young man took no notice of them, and only congratulated himself upon his good fortune. Now, when the wedding-day had at last come, and all the company were assembled and ready to assist at the ceremony, it seemed high time that the bowl should be removed from the head of the bride. She tried to take it off, but found, to her dismay, that it stuck fast, nor could her utmost efforts even succeed in moving it; and, when some of the relations persisted in trying to pull off the bowl, it uttered loud cries and groans as of pain.

The bridegroom comforted and consoled the maiden, and insisted that they should go on with the ceremony without more ado.

And with the bowl fell a shower of precious stones: pearls, diamonds, rubies, and emeralds, which had been hidden beneath it.

And now came the moment when the wine cups were brought in, and the bride and bridegroom must drink together the "three times three," in token that they were now become man and wife. Hardly had the bride put her lips to the *saké* cup when the wooden bowl burst with a loud noise, and fell in a thousand pieces upon the floor. And with the bowl fell a shower of precious stones, pearls, and diamonds, rubies, and emeralds, which had been hidden beneath it, besides gold and silver in abundance, which now became the marriage portion of the maiden.

But what astonished the wedding guests more even than this vast treasure was the wonderful beauty of the bride, made fully known for the first time to her husband and to all the world. Never was there such a merry wedding, such a proud and happy bridegroom, or such a lovely bride.

The Tea-Kettle

LONG AGO, as I've heard tell, there dwelt at the temple of Morinji, in the Province of Kotsuke, a holy priest.

Now there were three things about this reverend man. First, he was wrapped up in meditations and observances and forms and doctrines. He was a great one for the Sacred Sutras, and knew strange and mystical things. Then he had a fine exquisite taste of his own, and nothing pleased him so much as the ancient tea ceremony of the *Cha-no-yu;* and for the third thing about him, he knew both sides of a copper coin well enough and loved a bargain.

None so pleased as he when he happened upon an ancient tea-kettle, lying rusty and dirty and half-forgotten in a corner of a poor shop in a back street of his town.

"An ugly bit of old metal," says the holy man to the shopkeeper. "But it will do well enough to boil my humble drop of water of an evening. I'll give you three *rin* for it." This he did and took the kettle home, rejoicing; for it was of bronze, fine work, the very thing for the *Cha-no-yu.*

A novice cleaned and scoured the tea-kettle, and it came out as pretty as you please. The priest turned it this way and that, and upside down, looked into it, tapped it with his fingernail. He smiled. "A bargain," he cried, "a bargain!" and rubbed his hands. He set the ket-

47

tle upon a box covered over with a purple cloth, and looked at it so long that first he was fain to rub his eyes many times, and then to close them altogether. His head dropped forward and he slept.

And then, believe me, the wonderful thing happened. The tea-kettle moved, though no hand was near it. A hairy head, with two bright eyes, looked out of the

Four brown and hairy paws appeared, and a fine bushy tail.

spout. The lid jumped up and down. Four brown and hairy paws appeared, and a fine bushy tail. In a minute the kettle was down from the box and going round and round looking at things.

"A very comfortable room, to be sure," says the tea-kettle.

Pleased enough to find itself so well lodged, it soon began to dance and to caper nimbly and to sing at the top of its voice. Three or four novices were studying in the next room. "The old man is lively," they said, "only hark to him. What can he be at?" And they laughed in their sleeves.

Heaven's mercy, the noise that the tea-kettle made! Bang! bang! Thud! thud! thud!

The novices soon stopped laughing. One of them slid aside the *kara-kami* and peeped through.

"Arah, the devil and all's in it!" he cried. "Here's the master's old tea-kettle turned into a sort of a badger. The gods protect us from witchcraft, or for certain we shall be lost!"

"And I scoured it not an hour since," said another novice, and he fell to reciting the Holy Sutras on his knees.

A third laughed. "I'm for a nearer view of the hobgoblin," he said.

So the lot of them left their books in a twinkling, and gave chase to the tea-kettle to catch it. But could they come up with the tea-kettle? Not a bit of it. It danced and it leapt and it flew up into the air. The novices rushed here and there, slipping upon the mats. They grew hot. They grew breathless.

"Ha, ha! Ha, ha!" laughed the tea-kettle; and "Catch me if you can!" laughed the wonderful tea-kettle.

Presently the priest awoke, all rosy, the holy man.

"And what's the meaning of this racket," he says, "disturbing me at my holy meditations and all?"

"Master, master," cry the novices, panting and mopping their brows, "your tea-kettle is bewitched. It was a badger, no less. And the dance it has been giving us, you'd never believe!"

"Stuff and nonsense," says the priest. "Bewitched?

Not a bit of it. There it rests on its box, good quiet thing, just where I put it."

Sure enough, so it did, looking as hard and cold and innocent as you please. There was not a hair of a badger near it. It was the novices that looked foolish.

"A likely story indeed," says the priest. "I have heard of the pestle that took wings to itself and flew away, parting company with the mortar. That is easily to be understood by any man. But a kettle that turned into a badger—no, no! To your books, my sons, and pray to be preserved from the perils of illusion."

That very night the holy man filled the kettle with water from the spring and set it on the *hibachi* to boil for his cup of tea. When the water began to boil—

"Sorcery!" cried the priest. "Black magic! Help! Help! Help!"

"Ai! Ai!" the kettle cried. "Ai! Ai! The heat of the Great Hell!" And it lost no time at all, but hopped off the fire as quick as you please.

"Sorcery!" cried the priest. "Black magic! A devil! A devil! A devil! Mercy on me! Help! Help! Help!" He was frightened out of his wits, the dear good man. All the novices came running to see what was the matter.

"The tea-kettle is bewitched," he gasped. "It was a badger, assuredly it was a badger. It both speaks and leaps about the room."

"Nay, master," said a novice, "see where it rests upon its box, good quiet thing."

And sure enough, so it did.

"Most reverend sir," said the novice, "let us all pray to be preserved from the perils of illusion."

The priest sold the tea-kettle to a tinker and got for it twenty copper coins.

"It's a mighty fine bit of bronze," says the priest. "Mind, I'm giving it away to you, I'm sure I cannot tell what for." Ah, he was the one for a bargain! The tinker was a happy man and carried home the kettle. He turned it this way and that, and upside down, and looked into it.

"A pretty piece," says the tinker. "A very good bargain." And when he went to bed that night he put the kettle by him, to see it first thing in the morning.

He awoke at midnight and fell to looking at the kettle by the bright light of the moon.

Presently it moved, though there was no hand near it.

"Strange," said the tinker. But he was a man who took things as they came.

A hairy head, with two bright eyes, looked out of the kettle's spout. The lid jumped up and down. Four brown and hairy paws appeared, and a fine bushy tail. It came quite close to the tinker and laid a paw upon him.

"Well?" says the tinker.

"I am not wicked," says the tea-kettle.

"No," says the tinker.

"But I like to be well treated. I am a badger tea-kettle."

"So it seems," says the tinker.

"At the temple they called me names, and beat me and set me on the fire. I couldn't stand it, you know."

"I like your spirit," says the tinker.

"I think I shall settle down with you."

"Shall I keep you in a lacquer box?" says the tinker.

"Not a bit of it, keep me with you; let us have a talk now and again. I am very fond of a pipe. I like rice to eat, and beans and sweet things."

"A cup of *saké* sometimes?" says the tinker.

"Well, yes, now you mention it."

"I'm willing," says the tinker.

"Thank you kindly," says the tea-kettle. "And, as a beginning, would you object to my sharing your bed? The night has turned a little chilly."

"Not the least in the world," says the tinker.

The tinker and the tea-kettle became the best of friends. They ate and talked together. The kettle knew a thing or two and was very good company.

One day: "Are you poor?" says the kettle.

"Yes," says the tinker, "middling poor."

"Well, I have a happy thought. For a tea-kettle, I am out-of-the-way—really very accomplished."

"I believe you," says the tinker.

"My name is *Bumbuku-Chagama;* I am the very prince of Badger Tea-Kettles."

"Your servant, my lord," says the tinker.

"If you'll take my advice," says the tea-kettle, "you'll carry me round as a show; I really am out-of-the-way, and it's my opinion you'd make a mint of money."

"That would be hard work for you, my dear *Bumbuku*," says the tinker.

"Not at all; let us start forthwith," says the tea-kettle.

So they did. The tinker bought hangings for a theater, and he called the show *Bumbuku-Chagama*. How the people flocked to see the fun! For the wonderful and most accomplished tea-kettle danced and sang, and

*The people flocked to see the wonderful tea-kettle dance,
sing, and walk the tight rope.*

walked the tight rope as to the manner born. It played such tricks and had such droll ways that the people laughed till their sides ached. It was a treat to see the tea-kettle bow as gracefully as a lord and thank the people for their patience.

The *Bumbuku-Chagama* was the talk of the countryside, and all the gentry came to see it as well as the commonalty. As for the tinker, he waved a fan and took the money. You may believe that he grew fat and rich. He even went to Court, where the great ladies and the royal princesses made much of the wonderful tea-kettle.

At last the tinker retired from business, and to him the tea-kettle came with tears in its bright eyes.

"I'm much afraid it's time to leave you," it says.

"Now, don't say that, *Bumbuku,* dear," says the tinker. "We'll be so happy together now we are rich."

"I've come to the end of my time," says the tea-kettle. "You'll not see old *Bumbuku* any more; henceforth I shall be an ordinary kettle, nothing more or less."

"Oh, my dear *Bumbuku,* what shall I do?" cried the poor tinker in tears.

"I think I should like to be given to the temple of Morinji, as a very sacred treasure," says the tea-kettle.

It never spoke or moved again. So the tinker presented it as a very sacred treasure to the temple, and the half of his wealth with it.

And the tea-kettle was held in wondrous fame for many a long year. Some persons even worshiped it as a saint.

The Matsuyama Mirror

ALONG, long time ago, there lived in a quiet spot, a young man and his wife. They had one child, a little daughter, whom they both loved with all their hearts. I cannot tell you their names, for they have been long since forgotten, but the name of the place where they lived was Matsuyama, in the province of Echigo.

It happened once, while the little girl was still a baby, that the father was obliged to go to the great city, the capital of Japan, upon some business. It was too far for the mother and her little baby to go, so he set out alone, after bidding them good-by, and promising to bring them home some pretty present.

The mother had never been further from home than the next village, and she could not help being a little frightened at the thought of her husband taking such a long journey, and yet she was a little proud too, for he was the first man in all that countryside who had been to the big town where the King and his great lords lived, and where there were so many beautiful and curious things to be seen.

At last the time came when she might expect her husband back, so she dressed the baby in its best clothes, and herself put on a pretty blue dress which she knew her husband liked.

You may fancy how glad this good wife was to see him come home safe and sound, and how the little girl clapped her hands, and laughed with delight, when she

saw the pretty toys her father had brought for her. He
had much to tell of all the wonderful things he had seen
upon the journey, and in the town itself.

"I have brought you a very pretty thing," said he to
his wife. "It is called a mirror. Look and tell me what you
see inside." He gave to her a plain, white, wooden box,

"I have brought you a very pretty thing," said he to his wife.
"It is called a mirror."

in which, when she had opened it, she found a round
piece of metal. One side was white like frosted silver,
and ornamented with raised figures of birds and flow-
ers, the other was bright as the clearest crystal. Into it
the young mother looked with delight and astonishment, for, from its depths was looking at her with part-
ed lips and bright eyes, a smiling, happy face.

"What do you see?" again asked the husband,
pleased at her astonishment, and glad to show that he
had learned something while he had been away. "I see
a pretty woman looking at me, and she moves her lips
as if she was speaking, and—dear me, how odd, she has
on a blue dress just like mine!" "Why, you silly woman,
it is your own face that you see," said the husband,
proud of knowing something that his wife didn't know.
"That round piece of metal is called a mirror, in the
town everybody has one, although we have not seen
them in this country place before."

The wife was charmed with her present, and for a few
days could not look into the mirror often enough, for
you must remember, that as this was the first time she
had seen a mirror, so, of course, it was the first time she
had ever seen the reflection of her own pretty face. But
she considered such a wonderful thing far too precious
for everyday use, and soon shut it up in its box again,
and put it away carefully among her most valued trea-
sures.

Years passed on, and the husband and wife still lived
happily. The joy of their life was their little daughter,
who grew up the very image of her mother, and who
was so dutiful and affectionate that everybody loved
her. Mindful of her own little passing vanity on finding
herself so lovely, the mother kept the mirror carefully
hidden away, fearing that the use of it might breed a
spirit of pride in her little girl.

She never spoke of it, and as for the father, he had forgotten all about it. So it happened that the daughter grew up as simple as the mother had been, and knew nothing of her own good looks, or of the mirror which would have reflected them.

But by and by a terrible misfortune happened to this happy little family. The good, kind mother fell sick; and, although her daughter waited upon her day and night, with loving care, she got worse and worse, until at last there was no hope but that she must die.

When she found that she must so soon leave her husband and child, the poor woman felt very sorrowful, grieving for those she was going to leave behind, and most of all for her little daughter.

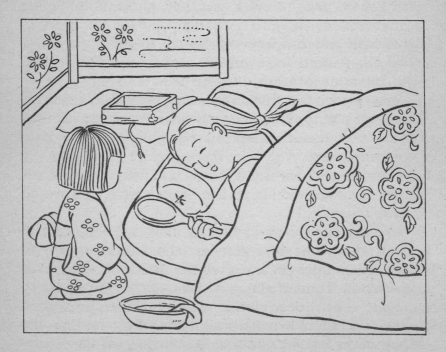

She took the mirror from its hiding-place and gave it to her daughter.

She called the girl to her and said: "My darling child, you know that I am very sick: soon I must die, and leave your dear father and you alone. When I am gone, promise me that you will look into this mirror every night and every morning: there you will see me, and know that I am still watching over you." With these words she took the mirror from its hiding-place and gave it to her daughter. The child promised, with many tears, and so the mother, seeming now calm and resigned, died a short time after.

Now this obedient and dutiful daughter never forgot her mother's last request, but each morning and evening took the mirror from its hiding-place, and looked in it long and earnestly. There she saw the bright and smiling vision of her lost mother. Not pale and sickly as in her last days, but the beautiful young mother of long ago. To her at night she told the story of the trials and difficulties of the day, to her in the morning she looked for sympathy and encouragement in whatever might be in store for her.

So day by day she lived as in her mother's sight, striving still to please her as she had done in her lifetime, and careful always to avoid whatever might pain or grieve her.

Her greatest joy was to be able to look in the mirror and say: "Mother, I have been today what you would have me to be."

Seeing her every night and morning, without fail, look into the mirror, and seem to hold converse with it, her father at length asked her the reason of her strange behavior. "Father," she said, "I look in the mirror every day to see my dear mother and to talk with her." Then she told him of her mother's dying wish, and how she had never failed to fulfil it. Touched by so much simplicity, and such faithful, loving obedience, the father shed tears of pity and affection. Nor could he find it in his heart to tell the child that the image she saw in the mirror was but the reflection of her own sweet face, by constant sympathy and association becoming more and more like her dead mother's day by day.

THE END